THE WALLOPING WINDOW-BLIND

THE WALLOPING WINDOW-BLIND

By CHARLES E. CARRYL

Illustrated by TED RAND

~ ~ ~ ~

Arcade Publishing : *New York*
LITTLE, BROWN AND COMPANY

A capital ship for an ocean trip
Was the *Walloping Window-Blind*;
No wind that blew dismayed her crew
Or troubled the captain's mind.

The man at the wheel was taught to feel
Contempt for the wildest blow,
And it often appeared, when the weather had cleared,
That he'd been in his bunk below.

So, blow ye winds, heigh-ho,
A-roving I will go;
I'll stay no more on England's shore,
So let the music play;

I'm off for the morning train,
I'll cross the raging main,
I'm off for my love with a boxing glove
Ten thousand miles away.

The boatswain's mate was very sedate,
Yet fond of amusement, too;
And he played hopscotch with the starboard watch
While the captain tickled the crew.

And the gunner we had was apparently mad,
For he sat on the after-rail
And fired salutes with the captain's boots
In the teeth of the booming gale.

The captain sat on a commodore's hat
And dined, in a royal way,
On toasted pigs and pickles and figs
And gummery bread, each day.

But the cook was Dutch and behaved as such,
For the food that he gave the crew
Was a number of tons of hot-cross buns
Served up with sugar and glue.

And we all felt ill as mariners will
On a diet that's cheap and rude;
And we shivered and shook as we dipped the cook
In a tub of his gluesome food.

Then nautical pride we laid aside,
And we cast the vessel ashore
On the Gulliby Isles, where the Poohpooh smiles,
And the Anagazanders roar.

Composed of sand was that favored land,
And trimmed with cinnamon straws;
And pink and blue was the pleasing hue
Of the Tickletoeteaser's claws.

And we sat on the edge of a sandy ledge
And shot at the whistling bee,
While the Binnacle-bats wore waterproof hats
As they danced in the sounding sea.

On rubagub bark, from dawn till dark,
We fed till we all had grown
Uncommonly shrunk — when a Chinese junk
Came up from the torriby zone.

She was stubby and square, but we didn't much care,
And we cheerily put to sea;
And we left the crew of the junk to chew
The bark of the rubagub tree.

∿ A NOTE FROM THE ILLUSTRATOR ∿

I've always enjoyed Charles Carryl's poem "The Walloping Window-Blind" and felt it would make a wonderful children's book. The poem was originally published in 1885 in Carryl's fantasy adventure for children entitled *Davy and the Goblin*. It has been reprinted in poetry anthologies and even adapted as a song for college glee clubs in Dick and Beth Best's collection *Song Fest*, now out of print. The chorus of the song is itself an attractive subject for illustration, and I've included it (in italics) with the text of the poem. Carryl aficionados may notice two other changes. In both cases, I've altered text slightly to make it more amenable to illustration. For the singers among you, the music and lyrics for the song are printed on the back endpaper.

To Elinor MacDonald, the song sleuth

Library of Congress Cataloging-in-Publication Data

Carryl, Charles E. (Charles Edward), 1841-1920.
    The walloping window-blind / by Charles E. Carryl ; illustrated by Ted Rand. — 1st ed.
        p.   cm.
    Summary: An illustrated version of the nonsense poem about an extraordinary ship and the follies and misadventures of her madcap crew.
    ISBN 1-55970-154-4
    1. Children's poetry, American. [1. American poetry. 2. Nonsense verses.] I. Rand, Ted, ill. II. Title.
    PS1260.C65W3   1992
    811' .4 — dc20   91-24261

Published in the United States by Arcade Publishing, Inc., New York, a Little, Brown company
Published simultaneously in Canada by Little, Brown & Company (Canada) Limited
Printed in the United States of America / Designed by Marc Cheshire / WOR
1 3 5 7 9 10 8 6 4 2

A capital ship for an ocean trip
Was the *Walloping Window-Blind*;
No wind that blew dismayed her crew,
Or troubled the captain's mind.

The man at the wheel was made to feel
Contempt for the wildest blow-w-w,
Though it oft' appeared when the gale had cleared
That he'd been in his bunk below.

So, blow ye winds, heigh-ho,
A-roving I will go;
I'll stay no more on England's shore,
So let the music play-ay-ay;

I'm off for the morning train,
I'll cross the raging main,
I'm off for my love with a boxing glove
Ten thousand miles away.

The bo'sun's mate was very sedate,
Yet fond of amusement, too.
He played hopscotch with the starboard watch,
While the captain tickled the crew.

The gunner we had was apparently mad,
For he sat on the after ra-ai-ail,
And fired salutes with the captain's boots
In the teeth of a booming gale.

The captain sat on the commodore's hat,
And dined in a royal way
Off pickles and figs, and little roast pigs,
And gunnery bread each day.

The cook was Dutch and behaved as such,
For the diet he served the crew-ew-ew,
Was a couple of tons of hot-cross buns
Served up with sugar and glue.

Then we all fell ill as mariners will
On a diet that's rough and crude;
And we shivered and shook as we dipped the cook
In a tub of his gluesome food.

All nautical pride we cast aside,
And we ran the vessel asho-o-ore
On the Gulliby Isles, where the poopoo smiles,
And the rubbily ubdugs roar.

Composed of sand was that favored land,
And trimmed with cinnamon straws,
And pink and blue was the pleasing hue
Of the tickle-toe-teaser's claws.

We sat on the edge of a sandy ledge,
And shot at the whistling bee-ee-ee,
While the ring-tailed bats wore waterproof hats
As they dipped in the shining sea.

On rugbug bark from dawn till dark
We dined till we all had grown
Uncommonly shrunk, when a Chinese junk
Came up from the Torrible Zone.

She was chubby and square, but we didn't much care,
So we cheerily put to sea-ee-ea,
And we left all the crew of the junk to chew
On the bark of the rugbug tree.